A

Aura's Angel

A house of death mystery

Aura's Angel

A House of Death Mystery

By

Bobbie Kaald

KDP ISBN number: 9798852660503

Dedication

I dedicate this book to a love that I have lost but shall remain forever my secret.

Books by Bobbie Kaald

Sci-Fi
The Making of an Enemy
The Unmaking of an Enemy
The Enemies become Friends
The Enemies and Friends thru The Vortex
The Enemies and Friends Seek Utopia
Taisyd Revisited

Aaron adventure series
Aaron
Aaron and the Lake Animal
Aaron tells the truth about the Sasquatch
Aaron Learns about the Lake Animal
Aaron and the White Sturgeon
Aaron Finds Underground Seattle
Aaron Meets the Fort Casey Ghost
Aaron and the Ice Caves

Espionage Mystery Series
Felicia
Colin
Ezra

Historical Fiction
The Lost Branch vol. I
The Lost Branch vol. II
The Lost Branch vol. III
Cameo Memories vol. I

Stand alone for children
Lily
Spryte

Stand alone for teens
Saalinda

Serial killer mystery series
Death Comes with the Night—prequel to series
2500 Fruitdale Dr.
Sleeping Urges Awaken
The Family of Killers
Finding the Family of Killers
1450 Westwick Rd.

Paranormal
Aura's Ghost

Disclaimer

This is a fictional story written around a house from the town of Everett, Washington. None of these events ever occurred except in the imagination of the writer.

I hope you enjoy a slight trip into the realm of angels.

Table of Contents

Chapter One

Some say that the plague was over, and we were free to go out. I didn't feel free. Sometimes I just went out and pretended I never had agoraphobia that I caught from the social media. I never read social media before being locked down by the plague. I never even read celebrity smut papers before, either.

I grew up in a one income family. I didn't really consider us poor. We always had food of a sort, and clothes to wear. True, my grandmothers made most of our clothes, but I liked them. I don't remember my sister complaining. Fact is, she hand sewed her entire trousseau when she was going to marry her beau.

I was accustomed to a Sunday drive as a way to have a mini vacation from childhood. I liked to take long drives any day of the week and watch the homes along the way. Most were new from when I was a child.

I had taught myself to look up because remarkably interesting homes were built with a view. The former owners must have had money at the time the house was built. It was difficult to tell if anyone lived there from looking up, but I got a good look at the beauty of the building.

Another thing that no one could know on many of these older buildings is whether or not they hid a basement. Sure, if there were windows hidden in the foundation a person knew there was a daylight basement. As for having a full basement, only the architect would know for certain without an in person look around.

I drove around looking for a familiar house from my childhood. My parents brought me here as a child. I don't know why. I guess my mother was fascinated with the house. It backed onto a hill, and it was there every time I drove by. Someday, I would write the house's story, but not today. Today I am only driving by.

I made the last turn and had to stop. There were police everywhere. Crime scene tape fluttered in a gentle breeze around the scene. Officers walked and ran into and out of my building. My building by right of the number of times I drove by.

I pulled over to the side and stopped the car. Watching the scene unfold, I was intrigued that there was such a response. This was a bedroom community without a care in the world. The response indicated that was no longer true. I sighed and prepared to leave when an officer knocked on my window.

Rolling down the window as if I knew this person, "I was just turning around, officer. I can see that you're busy." I looked him in the eye, and I could see that he was relieved to know that I had no intension of trying to get past him.

"That would be best. If you live here, I can ask." He answered but turned away and walked back to his post.

I briefly thought about saying that I did live here, but they would find out and then I would be in trouble. I didn't move my car for a few minutes as I tried to find a way to turn it around on this narrow residential road with sharp turns. I decided to just try and end up being embarrassed because I couldn't do it in one turn. All the driveways were full. Extra cars were parked everywhere, and I had been here so long that someone was now sitting parked on my bumper.

I guess the car's driver behind me was in a hurry because he began backing up as soon as he stopped. I watched to see how he did it, hoping to learn how I could get out. I saw him swing wildly into a driveway and barely stop. The next thing I knew, the car drove back the way he came.

That looked easy, but I had never been known for my backing-up skills. Just as I put my car into reverse, someone knocked on my window causing me to jump. My car jumped forward and knocked the barricade over. Quickly turning my car off for safety, I leaned on the steering wheel as my heart tried to jump out of my chest.

Weakly, I rolled my window down. "Did I hurt anyone?" I asked because I was afraid to look.

"No, but that was quite a show." A voice said next to my ear. "I am Detective Smith. Yes, Smith. The officer just told me you were here to take a drive?" He thought this was weird enough to ask questions for himself.

I made myself lift up off the steering wheel and look at him. "Yes, but I was trying to leave now that the car behind me left." I answered and looked out of the windshield to see if I hit anything substantial. It looked okay. "Maybe you could help me turn around?" I asked in the belief that if you don't ask, you don't get.

"I can have one of the men do that for you. Would you like to come in and tell me what you know about the house?" Detective Smith asked with a smile. He found over the years that his smile brought him mostly yes answers.

"I don't really know anything. I was just out for a drive. My name is Aura, I have always wanted to see inside." I began trying to form a plausible story without telling him that my father broke in many years ago so my mother could look around. The house was for sale then, too.

"Aura, why don't we go up to the house. Do you have your keys?" Detective Smith held out his hand and Aura filled his palm to overflowing with her large key ring and many keys. "Oh, which one?"

"It's the only car key." Aura points and turns toward their goal. "Is it a crime scene? Should I be allowed inside?" She asked in all innocence as she got out of the car. She was still covering up for her past.

"Walk with me and help me answer those very questions." Detective Smith smiled and began walking beside Aura. "If you have never been inside, why come this way for your drive?" Direct and to the point, he didn't have time to mess around with social niceties.

"It's because of a family story from my childhood. I have vague memories of the interior of the house but only through glass. My older sister and I spoke of coming here with our parents, long ago." Aura smiled at the detective as they walked along, but she needed to keep looking down at her feet due to the darkness of the shade making walking a very real problem for her.

"I see. How long ago was that?" Detective Smith knew this was a pointless exercise now but was committed to the end at this point.

"The mid fifties, I guess. I would have been four?" Aura was not clear on any of her past and had few actual memories. Most were things she was told or overheard.

They had reached the house and stood looking through the front window. "You don't have to do this, but we have questions. The coroner has already come and gone if you wish to know what to expect." Detective Smith volunteered this information as a way of helping her relax.

"There will be blood?" Aura just wanted to know, and asked as she stepped through and entered the front door of the home. She began shivering immediately on entering the house. The air was markedly cooler to her skin as she stepped inside, compared to the air outside that was hot on this seasonably warm day.

Detective Smith followed behind and remained silent. He simply chose instead to be silent and listen if she should speak.

Aura looked around and slowly walked through the large room in which she found herself. Before she could take two small steps, she noticed her breath was frostily apparent in front of her. "My breath! It is as if I was outside on a snowy day."

The Detective turned but said nothing. He had noticed this as well. Finally, he stopped at the basement door and spoke. "It is much warmer here." It was really much hotter here and he had tried to go into the basement, but it was too hot, and his skin was scorched when he tried.

"Is that why your face is all red?" Aura had noticed it but did not rudely bring it up on their first meeting. She walked as she spoke, eerily happier every moment that she spoke. "You're right it is warmer over here. Why is that?"

"When I open this door, a blast furnace of heat will answer your question, I think." The Detective pulled open the door and stood back. "No one has been able to go down the stairs to see why it is so hot. I am waiting for the Fire Department to see if they can bare the heat."

Aura jumped backward as the door opened and fell into the freezing temperature that she so recently left. "From the iceberg into the fire, then." She would never sleep again if she didn't find her answers now. Had she ever been down there? Stepping forward, she slowly forced herself to step by step descend into the depths of hell. Hell being her forgotten past.

"The heat has stopped. You are a brave woman, Aura." Detective Smith followed along behind her, feeling ashamed of not going first. He had never dreamed that she would not wait for the Fire Department as he said they were all awaiting their arrival.

Aura's vision was gradually improving as she descended into the dimly lit surroundings of this basement, now gone cold and a feeling of oppression surrounded her. Her head began to throb as a pounding headache began and her vision faded.

"I need to sit down." Aura sat on the last two steps as she spoke and hoped that her headache would end. She found her head felt too heavy and leaned over to hold it in her hands. Slowing her breathing, she felt the Detective step over her and stand in front of her successfully blocking her view of the darkness in front of them.

This seemed to help Aura's headache and she grabbed hold of the railing. Pulling herself up, she took the last step to keep from falling off the last step of the stairs. Looking at what little she could see; Aura didn't see any evidence of a recent crime. "I thought this was a crime scene. I don't see any blood."

"We sprayed down the area with luminal over here." Detective Smith stepped to the right as he spoke revealing a glowing florescent line of turquoise dots that spread out away from them.

"Is that from blood?" Aura's voice was weak and if it weren't so dark, she would look markedly whiter from a near faint. Her voice gone suddenly weak and breathless sounding.

"It isn't blood. We tested it, but any body fluid would glow. Even sweat." Detective Smith moved closer to Aura in case he had to catch her.

"Amniotic fluid?" Aura spoke this aloud without thinking and immediately wondered why.

"I guess so. Why would you ask that?" Smith asked her and found himself looking around the basement with a new insight.

"I don't know." Aura turned and started to walk back up the stairs. She was really sorry she ever decided to come here. Images started flashing through her mind so fast that she had to stop walking and grab the rail.

Seconds later Smith put his arm around her and encouraged her to finish walking up the steep stairs. He was worried that she would faint on the stairs and hurt herself falling down them. There were minimal furnishings left upstairs and Smith steered Aura to the closest chair to sit on until she felt recovered. "Just sit here until you feel that your strength has returned."

Detective Smith stood up and walked out of the house to check on his men. Once outside, he spoke to the man closest to the house. "I need the basement fingerprinted and illuminated. We need more information on this house."

Aura remained sitting mostly because her field of vision was blurred to the point of blocking out her surroundings. She had vague flashes of things that she should be able to identify but could not. The images themselves were also blurred and fast moving to the point of Aura beginning to feel vertigo and nausea. She leaned forward and put her hands over her eyes to no avail.

Turning around, the detective saw Aura leaning forward and rushed to keep her from falling. His running echoed through the house. "Miss, are you alright?" He had already forgotten her name. Did he ever know her name?

"Aura. My name is Aura and I need to leave this house of horrors." She tried to stand up but fell back onto the chair.

"Let me help you. We can go sit in a car away from here if you want." Smitty helped her up and they made their way out of the house carefully as Aura was not a steady walker at this point and Smitty was finding it difficult to keep her from falling.

At last, they were leaning against his car. "Thanks for bringing me out of that house. I'm feeling much better, now." Aura gave the detective a weak and fleeting smile. "I don't remember ever being in that house. I swear.

However, I kept getting flashes of images. From where, I don't know. My past, or stories of my past, or someone else's past."

"I knew something was happening in there. Are you okay now?" Smitty asked out of genuine concern. If anything happened to her, it would be his fault for taking her into the house.

"I am good, now." Aura answered and stood away from the car to prove it.

"Good, then, can I at least have your address and phone number for future questions." Smitty felt extremely self conscious about this question because Aura was a good-looking woman and he admitted to himself that he was attracted to her.

"Certainly." Aura gave him her requested information before continuing. She couldn't know that she would live to regret it. "Can I leave now and let you get on with whatever you are doing?"

"You may. When you get home, can you write down things you remember from these flashes? Anything can help more than you know." Detective Smith turned and walked back to the house. He had her information and would contact her later when he finished what he could here. This case was poorly investigated, if at all, and he would find out why if it were the last thing he did.

Chapter Two

Aura drove home slower than she had ever driven in her life. She was still shaking a little and should not have driven. Somehow, she made it into the house and collapsed on the sofa. She thought that sleep would come, but it did not. The flashes of images came back with a vengeance as if her eye lids were movie screens. After a short unknown period of time, Aura got up and took a hot shower.

Feeling refreshed and relaxed, she returned to the sofa and turned on the television. Perhaps she could find something on the news to tell her what they were doing mobbing her favorite house to drive by. The house had not relaxed her today and might never relax her again. There wasn't any local news on and so she vowed to try again around dinner time.

"I should have been more forceful about sharing what he knew. Well, he will be here for my notes, and I will ask for the truth before turning over what I don't know, then." Aura spoke aloud to reinforce her plan. She knew where her writing supplies were and found a notebook, she bought years ago for a college class. Grabbing a pen, Aura returned to the dining area for a spot to write and keep it available for additions.

Aura wrote in many bursts throughout the day and by bedtime felt good about the twenty pages of verbalized images that were now indelibly attached to the notebook. She realized that it was late and took her writing material and went to bed. She darkened her room as per her usual routine and placed the notebook on her bedside table.

Aura relieved herself and washed up before crawling into her old-fashioned bed. As she sank blissfully into the foam overlay, she pulled up her comforter to her chin and turned on her side. Barely closing her eyes, she heard a pounding coming from the front room. She ignored it. The house was dark, and they would get a hint and go away until a decent hour.

However, they didn't get a hint. The loud pounding resumed every few minutes. Aura sighed and threw off her covers and slowly slid off the edge of the bed. She stood in her nightgown looking around and grabbed a robe she recently purchased and never wore. Throwing it around herself, she managed to cover her nightgown before she reached the door.

"Who is it?" Aura yelled down to the door. She always stood to the side, having watched way too many movies, in the event of someone shooting through the door.

"It's Detective Smith." Smitty was already regretting his decision to come over instead of calling.

"Can you come back tomorrow?" Aura hoped she could persuade him.

"I guess that would be for the best." Smitty didn't want to argue his way in as she must be in her night clothes. He turned and walked away feeling ashamed of having come in the night.

Relief swept through Aura as she went over to the window and peeked out. Watching him walk away, Aura noticed that he had a slight limp. Now, she was feeling a lot of guilt. The man was here, answer his questions and give him the notes. She knocked on the window and then went over and opened the front door. "You might as well come in because I am not going to go to sleep after all of this. Coffee or tea?" Aura asked as she backed away to allow him entrance.

"None. I just wanted to know if you wrote down any of your images, for lack of a better word." Smitty was feeling like the stalker that he was and just wanted this over with. He shouldn't have come tonight. Somehow, he lost track of how late it was and how early some people went to bed. Ten p.m. was early for him.

"I did. If that's all you want, I can give you my notes and get back to bed." Aura was not known for tact and got straight to the guilt that he deserved.

"That will be fine." Smitty couldn't look her in the eye. He knew he had overstepped but continued to dig himself in even deeper.

Aura got up and went to get her notes. When she returned, she handed them over and looked at Smitty. "If you have questions, don't call before noon. I don't sleep well and won't be up early for an excellent reason." 'You waking me up,' she thought to herself.

"Thanks." Smitty took the notes she handed him and immediately got up to head for the door. Noon, he was awake by four am no matter what. He was having trouble digesting this information but would comply. He opened the door and closed in behind him. He heard it locking as he walked away. When he looked back as he got into his car, the house was dark. She really went to bed.

Chapter Three

Morning found Smitty back at the house. He was walking around the house trying to compare Aura's notes to what little was left inside of the house. He knew in his heart that it should have been a crime scene long ago, but no bodies were ever found. There were positive luminal reactions in more than twenty areas of the house. The terrible thing was that could be any body substance at this late date. No DNA was present and would be too degraded at this late date anyway.

Smitty covered the house thoroughly for about two hours but came up with nothing. Shaking his head, he put away the incomplete pictures and took out his notebook. He hoped that he had Aura's phone number in his book. He did and dialed it.

Aura answered immediately. "Hello."

"This is Smitty. I am at the house trying to make sense of these notes you gave me. Even though your sketches are good, I don't seem to be able to connect to anything at the house." He hated to admit fallibility but had no choice at this point.

"I'm not at home, but I am at a store about ten minutes away. Let me pay for my things and come to the house if that is what you want me to do." Aura didn't want this but one more time would be okay now that the shock was over, maybe.

"That would be great, if you wouldn't mind." Smitty said but heard the call terminate before he was done speaking. 'I guess that I wait.' Smitty muttered under his breath as he slowly shook his head, knowing that he deserved to wait.

It wasn't long before Aura drove slowly up to the house and pulled in behind Smitty's car. They were parked in a grassy strip next to the road to allow their cars to be as far off the road as possible and still let them open their door to get out. She got out as soon as the car stopped and walked up to the front door. "Did you bring the sketches?" She might want to look at them later.

"They are in the car." Smitty frowned at having to admit to not having the forethought to bring them up to the house.

"Get them because this is the last time that I go in there for you or anyone else." Aura knew she was being bossy but just couldn't help herself. She also knew that she would come back again if they needed her. She waited on the porch for Smitty to return with the sketches. "You hold on to them and I will let you know if I need them."

She turned to face the door as did Smitty. Smitty said nothing and intended to remain silent to allow her uninterrupted thinking. He hoped she would talk as new images came to her.

"You may open the door, now. My goosebumps need more company." Aura stood as if rooted to the spot and nodded. Her teeth were clenched to prevent them from chattering. She was very cold but pale and not blue from the cold of the out of doors.

Smitty opened the door and stood back. "I will follow you. Try to verbalize what you are seeing even if it isn't really there." He was told by his superiors that this was a waste of time, but it was his time to waste as he was off duty.

Aura nodded and took a few deep breaths before taking her first step inside. She would try to go into the basement, but the ominous oppressive atmosphere had been too much for her last time.

"I feel cold, and my hair is standing on end. I can see my breath as I exhale. I feel a deep fear but no visions, yet." Aura spoke slowly and carefully because her teeth were starting to chatter. "I feel many people around. I think most are women. They are afraid and hungry." By this time, she stopped in front of the door to the basement.

"Are you ready to have me open the door?" Smitty asked but remained behind her in case she fainted because he did not want her to hit her head or get injured in another way.

"I can do it. You will catch me if I need it?" Aura whispered as she opened the door. Immediately the visions came to her. "There are many women in the basement. They can't move because they are tied down to their beds. Some are pregnant, some are giving birth. Some are crying for their children." She slammed the door shut and began crying so violently that she collapsed into Smitty's arms on the floor.

"What did you see?" Smitty asked her quietly.

"Men were raping the women even the pregnant ones. When the babies are born, they are taken upstairs, and the women never see them again." Aura choked out between sobs.

"White slave trade and baby selling. Kidnapping and the works. This is worse than I imagined." Smitty helped her up and walked her out of the house.

"I need to go home. I can't help you anymore." Aura pulled away from him and walked to her car without looking back. She was glad that whoever had done these things was no longer here because she would come back and kill them.

Smitty watched her go. He might come up with questions later, but for now, he was off to the Property Tax Office for a file on this house and to start tracing the ownership over the years. He had no idea what decade he was talking about. If they had some remains, a coroner might be able to tell him when this horrible thing happened.

Chapter Four

It took more than a month, between other cases, for Smitty to make a list of former owners. Now he needed to track down their current addresses. This would not be an easy task with people moving thousands of miles away for a new job and the like.

One of the rare days of clear blue skies, Aura stopped into see if Smitty had found anything. He was not in. She left a message and laughed on her way out thinking of the last midnight visit and making bets with herself as to the chances of his visiting late tonight. Then again, he was probably thinking of her as crazy and would not come by again.

Aura made it to her car and began driving home. She had a bad habit of driving and allowing her mind to wander. This time it was not a suitable time to do this. When her mind came back to the now, she was driving past the house of murder and pain.

Aura had been just coasting, but a wave of fear hit her when she focused on the house. The car jumped forward as her foot must have gunned the gas and not the brake pedal. In her sudden frozen excitement, she braked hard and was overcome with a vision that took her sight from her.

Everything was white, but there were shadows. Shadows that looked like ghosts. People were coming and going a lot. Some of the people were carrying something. Aura could not breathe and wanted the vision to pass, but it grew stronger. When she was nearly passing out, a shadow passed through her, and she heard a baby cry. Finally, she could see again and breathe. She couldn't move yet and remained still while she regained regular breathing again.

Aura shivered. Whoever the ghosts were, they had been selling babies and she felt certain of that. Smitty was right. They were guilty of many heinous crimes all tied to sex and money. She shivered hard against the car seat again and found it difficult to take a complete breath. In fact, her chest felt tight, and she would have coughed if there was any air in her lungs to cough with.

Aura remembered that she was still inside of her car, and it was still running. For her sanity, she forced her eyes to look at the road ahead and tried to drive the car away. When the house was well behind her, she accelerated slowly and drove home wishing that she had not come back here.

When Aura arrived at her home, Smitty was there waiting for her. "I was told that you came to the station. I thought if it were that important, I would come here, and I have come here and been waiting for more than an hour."

"I went by the house and had another vision, and I didn't even go inside. I was in my car." Aura spoke slowly with her voice breaking and tear were leaking from her eyes and running down her cheeks.

"I think we should go in the house if that is okay with you." Smitty saw Aura shaking and turning visibly whiter than her usual tanned face.

Aura nodded and took Smitty's proffered hand because she wasn't certain if she could walk. When they arrived at her door, she had the key in her hand, but it shook too badly and Smitty had to unlock the door for her. No formalities were observed because they were practically old friends by now. They walked inside and Aura waved him to the refrigerator as she collapsed onto her couch.

Smitty did as he knew Aura wanted him to and looked in her refrigerator. He considered himself to be off duty and took the one and only beer in the door of the refrigerator. Going back into the room, he held up the beer. "This is the last beer. Did you want me to have it?"

"I don't drink, I bought it earlier for you if you ever came in." Aura was laying down with a hand over her eyes and spoke weakly. She answered only because it was the courteous thing to do.

Smitty took the only other chair in the room and sat down. He was off side of Aura, but he guessed it didn't matter. "You said you had a vision while sitting in your car?"

"Yes. I just drove by without meaning to and stopped in front of the house. Almost as soon as I stopped, the vision took over. Everything became white and foggy. Shadows came out of the house and stopped at the fence. Many shadows. Some were carrying what looked like babies. I heard babies crying and screams coming from the house. Women screaming in pain and fear or outrage." Her voice trailed off and she sat up. Looking Smitty in the eye, she continued. "I think that you are right. They were selling the babies and stealing them from the women. I think the women were prisoners in the basement and defiled many times to get them pregnant so they could sell the babies." By this time, she had to stop because she was sobbing uncontrollably. She laid back down and rolled into the couch with her back to Smitty.

Smitty went into the kitchen and put his unopened beer away. He wasn't thirsty anymore. He returned quietly to the living room and left by way of the front door. Closing the door softly, he turned the knob to assure himself that it would lock automatically. It did. He was going back to the station and continuing his research.

Chapter Five

Smitty sat behind his desk at the local police station. He could barely keep his eyes open even after a quad espresso. The days he spent at the library research room had yielded little added information. He knew when the house was built from the tax assessor's office. It was so old that the chain of ownership was lost during the transition to digital and the burning or burying of paper records.

Smitty did find the equivalent of a phone book for the fifties, but there was little prior to that. He settled for a list of owners from the date it was first built as accumulated from the property records. Reaching for the phone, he placed a call to Aura.

"Hello, this is Detective Smith." Smitty started off formally because he never knew if someone else would answer the phone. He listened and it was Aura's answering machine. He hung up without leaving a message. She was probably going to show up here anyway. She seemed to know when he was thinking about her.

Shaking his head, Smitty returned to researching possible leads. By the time he realized how late it was getting, his eyes were burning, and the lights were suddenly reduced. 'The night shift is already here.' He thought to himself and looked up, it was pitch black outside. The timers would be off for the next month because they changed daylight savings time to another month away.

Putting his things in order, and his files in the overnight drawer, Smitty stood up to leave. He was discouraged for a good reason because this cold case had heated up and then died before anything useful became known. He shook his head again and walked out to his car. Maybe he should go have dinner at 'Bud's' at least the food was decent.

While Smitty waited for his food, his mind sorted through the known information on this case. When the thought came to him, he stopped breathing and then started laughing. He was glad he didn't have his food yet.

Why it had not occurred to him that Aura's name might mean she had visions, he could not figure them out, but he wanted to meet her parents in the after life. He knew from somewhere that Aura's parents had passed, but he would have liked to ask them why they named her that.

Just then, his food came, and he thanked the server who brought it. He hadn't ordered much and was done in about five minutes. Getting up, he left copious money on the table and walked out. Now, he had to go to Aura's and ask her why she was named so. From what little he knew, women who had visions came from families of women who received visions. It was in the blood from long ago. Maybe through all time. He laughed at his left field thinking and consciously changed his train of thought. Now, he was only thinking of a way to kill these people without going to jail for it. Murder was definitely in his heart and mind. He knew from the past that he would not follow through, but he felt the need to revenge these women and children.

Chapter Six

As it turned out, Smitty went home. He had a sudden sense of bashfulness, for lack of a better word. Smitty would have her brought downtown if he had to, but he did not want to invade her privacy as he had done in the past. It wasn't good police work to go to the home of non-criminals. He didn't want Aura's neighbors to think she was a suspect in a crime of any kind. It wasn't a clever way to honey her into helping him.

After a quick shower, Smitty crashed on the bed and didn't even turn over until morning. As he slowly returned to consciousness, Smitty heard his phone ringing. "Hello." He managed to croak out of his dry mouth and throat. He listened for a minute before hanging up. As he was heading for the bathroom, he mumbled several unprintable soliloquies under his breath and then turned on the shower to warm up the water, while he peed in the toilet.

Putting clothes on while damp wasn't fun, but it was work and he had overslept. He poured coffee into his 'to go' mug and headed out the door. Aura had called the office and was waiting in their lobby at his Captain's request. He wasn't looking forward to her anger. Somehow, when she was angry at him, he imagined that she was hitting him because that is how he reacted to it.

He drove the speed limit because it was too embarrassing to get stopped for speeding and have to explain why he was speeding and show his identification. Finally, he arrived at the precinct and Smitty parked in the first spot designated for law enforcement. Getting out, he hurried over to the entrance feeling smuggish that he did not have to call her or go to her home, again.

Smitty walked with his head down and watching his own feet as was his habit after falling in front of a judge that he was about to testify for, a few months back. The door was opened by the man in front of him and he ducked through behind him. Next came the search, but he flashed his badge and was waived around. He took the stairs two at a time and barely turned the corner to visualize the department when he literally ran into Aura. He instinctively grabbed her to keep the two of them from falling.

Aura pushed his embrace away using her pent-up anger. “I have to go; you missed your chance.” She flew past Smitty and descended the stairs in a huff. ‘Why did he irritate her so much?’ Aura thought to herself as she exited the building.

Smitty didn’t say anything but followed her out of the building to the bus stop. He wondered briefly why she took the bus. “Captain said you had something that you wanted to talk over?”

Aura stopped and turned back to look at him. She had a blank look in her eyes, and he watched as they came into focus with the memory of what he was talking about. “Oh, it’s nothing. I had a flash this morning but decided that it wouldn’t interest you.” She turned again as the sound of a bus arriving came to her. It wasn’t her bus.

“I find everything you tell me to be remarkably interesting. Try me.” Smitty spoke softly, trying his best to be convincing.

Aura blushed at this innuendo from Smitty but chose to ignore him. “Some other time, maybe.”

“Sorry, but I need a new lead.” Smitty was being honest now and Aura picked up on that.

“I just wanted you to know that sounds are coming with the images now. I haven’t made any sense of them, but I thought that I might get something clearer if you came with me to the house or at least the two of us could cruise by, slowly." Aura looked Smitty in the eye as she spoke to assess his emotional response. His actual verbal response might differ, but emotional responses told her everything.

"I can give you a ride home via the house in question. Maybe you might even want dinner. We could eat in the car and clarify the new sensory overload?" Smitty continued speaking softly with a seductive tone that he didn't realize was there. When Aura nodded, he walked slowly toward his car to make certain she was following. She was.

Aura let herself in and waited for Smitty to start the car. She neither spoke nor looked at him, lost in her own thoughts. Smitty took his cue from her and drove away from the police station at the speed limit and looking straight ahead. He knew the way to the house as did Aura. As they closed the distance to their house in question, Aura stiffened, and the color slowly drained from her face. She was gripping the door handle so hard that her knuckles were turning white.

Smitty made the first turn and began hearing whispering coming from Aura. He dared not look at her because she would be embarrassed if tears were streaming down her face. He could feel the tension building in the air around them because it always did when she was having a vision. The hair on his body was standing up and he felt like sparks were snapping on his skin. He tried to ignore the tension and continued driving cautiously to keep the car on the road.

On the last turn before being able to see the house, Smitty unconsciously swerved the car to miss something he thought he saw, but there was nothing there. He swore too loudly and hoped Aura didn't hear it because he didn't want her concentration broken. She didn't hear him, but her whispering was getting louder. It was nearly loud enough to understand the word or words.

He pulled the car over as far as possible and stopped for everyone's safety. Getting out, Smitty walked around and opened Aura's door. She didn't look at him. He saw that her belt wasn't buckled, and he pulled her gently from the car. Walking with his arm around her waist, they made slow progress toward the house and up the walk to the door.

Bizarrely, the door was wide open. Smitty was certain that he locked it before he left. Aura took another step, and they were inside. Smitty kept his eyes moving, watching for a human predator. Something he could shoot and kill.

Smitty held Aura up and walked over to the chair that was thankfully still there and sat her down on it. Some twenty minutes later, Aura came out of it. "Can we leave, and I will tell you what I can on the way back home."

"Gladly, do you need help?" Smitty helped her stand, but she shook him off and walked slowly out of the house.

Once they were in the car and leaving, Aura began to talk. "I still don't know much more, but clearly, they were stealing the babies and selling them. They may have killed the women and buried them somewhere. Maybe you should x-ray the property. The whispering didn't tell me any names, sorry."

"We just have to keep working on this mystery. Something should come up." Smitty responded in his usual rote fashion but was not feeling confident that anything would work. "I think we could get some sort of radar and look into the ground. Is that what your are talking about?"

"Something to look for bodies buried long ago." Aura said this and shivered. Tears started running down her cheeks and she didn't care who knew it.

"After I get you home, I will look into it and this I promise you." Smitty was concerned about her health. "I want you to stay away from here and let me come to you. This effects you in a bad way and I don't want to have anything happen to you just because you want to help."

Aura nodded and leaned back to rest. Her eyes were closed, and she might be sleeping lightly. She took a shuttering breath and remained quiet.

Chapter Seven

Over the next couple of weeks, Officer Smitty managed to get a crew over to the property who claimed to have ground penetrating radar. He was not thrilled with the bill that came with the crew and was certain his boss wouldn't be either.

Only two men came and hauled out some rickety looking equipment. Smitty had to leave the area while he calmed himself down. He was certain these guys were quacks, and he might have to pay the bill himself. Maybe he could take out a loan with some unscrupulous loan shark.

After he calmed himself down and pasted a smile back on his face, Smitty walked over to the two men. "Have you any idea how long this will take?"

"We are ready to start now. How much of this area do you want us to cover?" The owner of the business answered him, the same voice Smitty heard on the phone. Larou was the name on the truck.

"I want you to start around the edges and look for any sign of a body, maybe it might be small." Smitty was out of his comfort zone and found himself short of words and stuttered some as he spoke.

"Really? I don't know but we can try." Larou answered and let his voice trail off.

The two men began dragging their contraption around and talking to each other as they stopped every few steps and looked at a small screen. Then, they started again. Once in a while they put a marker into the ground.

Smitty left them to their work and returned to his car. His left-over cold coffee was all that he had, and he took it out and sipped on it as he leaned against the car. This was definitely the worst idea that he ever came up with and all because some pretty femme fetale suggested there could be bodies buried here.

Smitty wanted to leave and come back later but maybe they would find something, and he should be there when they did. He really wanted to go to the library and start reading some microfilmed old newspapers. His captain suggested this, and it was his next wild guess.

Smitty barely finished his whiney thought when the men called him over. "Sir, I think if you dig anywhere, you will find what you need. I can recommend an archeologist if the buried item is incredibly old." Larou stated and stood there awaiting a response because as far as he was concerned, they were done here. He didn't like to over bill because he didn't get a return booking, so to speak.

"Really, got a shovel?" Smitty took his coat off and laid it on the porch before grabbing the shovel. "Best guess?" As he put the shovel to the point of Larou's boot toe, he spoke again. "Oh, you may as well pack it up and call me at the office if you discover a phone number for the archeologist."

The two men began to pack up their equipment and haul the makeshift machine back to their van. As they walked away, the sound of a bone snapping reached their ears and hurried their packing. Larou would never send a bill for what he now found a gruesome job that would haunt his days.

Chapter Eight

Smitty was way out of his area of expertise. He did not bring in an archeology team. He did go to his Captain and was told to send over a crime scene team of technicians. He was happy to do that but continued to check in on the scene twice a day as a plan.

Over the last month, fifty babies remains, and twenty-five adult skeletons had been recovered. The adult remains were all women and the infants appeared to be newborns. This sickened Smitty to the point of losing his ability to concentrate.

Today, Smitty was heading back to the library research room. He needed to know who owned that house and when. He needed to compile a list by time sequence before the morgue would tell him what years these babies and mother's were buried.

As Smitty entered the library, the employee's all in their own way noticed his arrival. The woman in charge of the research room arrived at the same time as he did to unlock the door for him. "I pulled some material that I think might help you." She smiled at him and entered first as he motioned for her to proceed.

Smitty followed behind the young woman, all employees were becoming younger than he was. He noticed this increasingly each day that he worked on his job. She led him to her desk and turned as she pointed to three volumes. "I think these will be a good start. Let me know if you need more help." With that, she turned and left him alone to think as he researched.

Several hours later, Smitty gathered up his notes. He didn't have what he needed but he did have three names and a date that they lived in the house. If they owned it, he would have to check at the title company. For that, he needed a court order, unless he got lucky, and it was considered public domain.

Since Smitty was only a block away from the title company closest to him, he decided to walk over and ask. At least he would know if he needed a court order. It took a few minutes, but he arrived at the front door, looking at the times printed on the door, he realized they closed in less than thirty minutes. Just enough time for his question.

The woman receptionist just waved him through and Smitty walked along reading the signs and looking for the title search room. He didn't find one but stopped at the nearest desk.

"Excuse me, I just have a quick question." Smitty looked around but didn't really see anyone. Maybe he would have to come back tomorrow after all.

He was just getting ready to leave when a woman approached carrying a pile of papers. "Detective, Aura called and said to expect you. These are copies of the records for the house that is bothering her. I'm her sister and never ask questions when she calls. I have gotten used to this. It doesn't happen often, but she means it when she calls." The woman smiled and then left Smitty to his own devices.

Shocked, Smitty picked up the papers and hurried to leave before she could change her mind. If only his whole life could be this easy. He was glad to know that Aura had a sister who worked here. It might help him in the future.

Smitty jumped in his car and drove straight to his office. Taking the papers with him, he nearly ran for his desk, but he almost fell by tripping on the curb. After that he walked into the building and managed to get to his desk without collapsing. His heart was beating so fast that he dared not drink any coffee. He certainly didn't need any chemicals to speed up his heart.

When he felt a little calmer, Smitty made certain he had his yellow notepad and a pen for notes before starting to look into all this information. There were pages and pages with nothing pertinent on the pages. He was nearly ready to give up when the address appeared. There was a note attached that they changed the address for some reason. Now, he turned all of the pages he had just read back over and began looking at them as if it were the same address because he guessed it was.

Smitty began to smile as he started over on the files given to him by Aura's sister. He printed the names on his pad. Owner's name, wife, children's names. There were many children listed although many of them had a D. next to their name as if they died while living there. He only got through five pages before his eyes wouldn't stay open anymore.

It was hours past the end of his shift when Smitty locked these precious files in his desk. He staggered out of the building and said goodnight to the man at the front desk. The guard would sign him out. Briefly, he wondered if he was safe to drive home. No matter, he got into his car and started her up like always. He may have dozed off because he soon found himself parked in front of his home. Driving around the back, he parked it in his usual spot and got out, locking the door behind himself. He wandered up to the front door and unlocked it. Opening the door, he found the silence unusual because he had not heard it in days. Locking the house door, he headed for bed. Tomorrow was the start of an exceedingly long week; he knew this for certain from the current information that he had recently read over.

Chapter Nine

The next morning found Aura still in bed at two in the afternoon. The trip to the house of ill omens had taken it's toll on her emotions. When she got up, she was very shaky even after all of this time. She had indeed lost track of time, but Smitty hadn't been by either. Vaguely, she wondered what Smitty was doing.

For his part, Smitty was terribly busy. Whenever he thought they had found all of the remains, there were more. The lists of owners of the house that he had, were never heard of before all this and it was growing. Not only that, somehow, he had to find the names of the renters who lived there from time to time. To say that he was frustrated would be a major understatement.

Smitty knew now that this thankless job was never ending and a hopeless waste of time. He would never know who was responsible unless one of Aura's visions told him a name. At least he needed to know if it was a man or a woman or a gang. Smiling, Smitty pictured Aura having a vision of a dark angel giving her the names from God's book of the dead. Overcome with his own dark comedy, Smitty laughed out loud and for a long time.

Everyone stopped what they were doing and turned to look at Smitty and then shook their heads. They all had bets on when Smitty would lose his mind. Only one of them was smiling a great deal because this could count as a win.

Aura was about to step into the shower when the vision overtook her. The house was in the background, but she could barely see it from all of the mist covering it. The voice was there but barely loud enough for her to hear the words.

"Nothing to be afraid of. Only the dead are left here. The living have moved away and are passing on their skills to others. You must stop them. I have killed the evil within the house, but the living have carried it with them in their minds. They must be stopped by the word of God. I am his messenger and will be with you always."

Aura turned to look where the voice seemed to come from and saw a feathery shadow turning translucent as a bright light came up behind him to show the image of a dark angel surrounded by the light. With that, the angel lifted his wings and rose above her and then over her. She felt something like a gentle kiss on her left cheek. She could not help but smile as the feeling of love and gentleness filled her and remained with her until long after the light was gone.

Aura took a quick shower and dressed in clean clothes. Grabbing her purse and car keys, she left in quest of Smitty. She needed to tell him what the angel said. She didn't really know what to make of it, but she knew that Smitty needed to know about the vision. She wasn't certain it was a vision, but it was something and it might help Smitty.

Chapter Ten

Smitty wasn't in the office when Aura arrived. She left her number for him to call. Feeling incredibly sad for the first time in many years, Aura drove home.

In the back of her mind, Aura continued to feel the presence of the dark angel and the wing tips brushing her cheeks as he flew away. She found herself smiling at the memory, happy again for the first time in her memory.

Aura drove home without meaning to. 'Darn, I was going to the grocery story.' She nearly started the car again, but decided she could go tomorrow. Instead, she got out of the car and went into her house. Her happiness was beginning to fade, and she didn't want that to happen.

Once inside the house, Aura locked herself inside and flopped down on the couch. Her heart was beginning to race for no reason, and she needed to let it rest. Closing her eyes, she waited for her memory of the happiness to return. Sleep overcame her as her thoughts began to float away.

Seemingly seconds later, Aura was awakened suddenly. Her brain wasn't ready to wake up yet. She couldn't make out why she was wanted or where she was, even. Reality came back to her slowly as she finally focused on the reason that she woke up. Some rude person was knocking on her front door and calling her name. No one but Smitty knew her name, that she knew of.

"Coming." Aura's voice was not strong, and her mouth was bone dry like skeletal remains in the desert. Her voice came out in a broken whisper.

Aura finally reached the door as this person knocked again. She threw open the door, Aura stood there glaring at....Smitty. "I just knew it was you. Do you need me, really?"

"I'm sorry, I didn't know you were sleeping. I needed to find out why you came to the office. The captain said that you came to see me." Smitty was getting ready for her to unload on him verbally and loudly.

"Did you bring me a soda?" Aura saw that he was holding a bag and thus didn't come empty handed. She stepped back and walked away from the door and smiled when she heard Smitty enter and shut the door.

The two took their now customary seats and waited for the other to go first. A laughable social situation, but Smitty broke the ice. "Yes, I brought a six pack of pop and a beer for me."

"Well, let me have my share and we can relax while I tell you the latest update." Aura said and laughed as she reached out and took her sodas. She opened one and took a drink before continuing. "I've been seeing a dark angel in the shadows of the mist. He says there was a dark presence in the house that he got rid of. It made all of the occupants do things, but the living have moved on. Does that make any sense to you?" She stopped talking and took another drink while Smitty absorbed what she just said.

"That is interesting. Did you feel threatened by this vision?" Smitty didn't know what else to say because he still didn't know enough about her abilities.

Aura wasn't expecting this question and didn't answer for a time as she sat frozen in mid response, and she stared at Smitty. "I guess that I can say, no. It was more of a loving and supportive feeling."

"Well, maybe if you see him again, you could ask for names and addresses or at least where they moved to? Just asking." Smitty wondered at this new revelation of Aura's. He wondered about all of it really but tried to keep it to himself. "Well, I should go. You were already asleep and must be tired. Tomorrow, I will be at the office trying to make sense of the research that your sister gave me. Thanks, by the way, for telling her to get me these names." He got up as he finally remembered that he had yet to thank her, and then walked to the door.

Aura followed his line of thinking and walked with him to the door. "She was happy to do it. She said that work had been slow with the building freeze and all." Smitty smiled and let himself out. Aura locked the door behind him and took their left-over mess to the kitchen before retiring for the night. She smiled as she thought about Smitty. It had been a long for her since her last unfortunate date. She could really pick the bad seed and she knew it.

Chapter Eleven

Aura awakened from the bliss of dreamless sleep, at last. Feeling revived from the last few months, she got up and worked on her morning routine. Once she was showered and fed, she left the house for a long walk to breathe in the untainted air of a city free of smog for once.

Happy and smiling, Aura innocently walked along the way on a sidewalk being careful not to trip over the uneven surface. She had a history of tripping on just about anything and was walking along watching her feet more than she should. After six blocks, she turned around and returned to her home intending on going grocery shopping.

When she arrived, Aura's mood changed as she saw that Smitty's car was parked in front of her home. Her car was also there but he was standing next to it, awaiting her arrival. "I was in a good mood, what do you want? I have nothing new to tell you." She wanted to say, leave me alone but decided to hear him out.

"I was out this way and wanted to save you a trip if there was more news for me to hear." Smitty spoke slowly as he could sense that his presence irritated her.

Aura was preparing to answer in the negative when she felt the glowing warmth of her new guardian envelope her in his presence. "He is here." She announced as if Smitty would know what she meant.

"Are you having a vision?" Smitty didn't think so because she wasn't acting as if she were about to faint, again.

"No, the angel is here. Angel, where did the bad people move to?" Aura spoke softly and with doubt at what she named the perpetrators. She should have said perpetrators, but she didn't think the angel would call them that.

'East' was the word floating in the wind as if all could hear. Aura looked at Smitty in the eyes and saw him nod.

"Wenatchee or further?" Aura knew this was a long shot but smiled at the answer.

'As you have said. Now go.' With that his presence faded into nothingness and only a slight breeze marked his passing.

"You want to go to Wenatchee with me?" Smitty asked just to be nice, fully expecting her to say no.

"I can be ready in an hour." Aura said as she turned to walk toward her front door.

"Give me two hours to get approval and be here to pick you up." Smitty grinned as he walked away. He thought he would have to go alone. His charm must be effective on Aura because it wasn't effective on anyone else.

Three hours later, the two "co-detectives" were entering the slow zone on the way across the pass. Aura had never been here or anywhere else away from home and watched the scenery the entire way. She made comments about everything and wanted to stop to see the falls, but they didn't have time.

Eventually, Aura dozed off after they crept through the local Bavarian town. The new divided highway after Blewitt Pass was like a freeway and she was bored. When the car slowed as they entered Wenatchee, she awakened. "Do you know where the station is?"

"They said to just drive straight ahead as the new road goes off to the right. We will find it, even if we have to drive through several times." Smitty didn't mind because it gave him the lay of the land. So far, he had not seen a patrol car and that worried him, somewhat. "Perhaps the officers are awaiting our arrival at the station. We may see several cars in front."

"That little to do?" Aura spoke mostly to herself but saw Smitty nod out of the corner of her eye. She wondered, in passing, if the angel would appear over here or if he could only go to the house, and her house of course.

They were nearly at the end of the buildings when they spotted two police cars parked in front of a building and Smitty pulled in next to one and turned the car off. "This must be the place."

"I guess so." Aura was shocked at the small-town western feel of this town. She had lived on the West Coast her entire life and was unaware that the rest of the state was somewhat of a large bedroom community. When she got out, she shut her own door and followed Smitty because she was lost, and he looked like he knew somewhat where they were going. She was hoping that he wasn't as lost as she was.

Smitty realized he was several feet in front of Aura and stopped to wait for her. "Sorry, I guess that I forgot my manners." When she was caught up to him, he turned and walked with her up to the door and opened it for her to go inside and then he followed. His manners had returned, for good he hoped.

Hours later, they emerged from the police station. Neither was speaking or smiling. Aura walked slowly over to the car with a crushing headache from the depression she was now in. What they learned here was new to both of them and opened her eyes even further with the truth of the world that she lived in. She felt lucky to have lived this long and not run into the criminal life that pervaded the world around her without her knowledge.

Once they were in the car, Aura turned and spoke to Smitty. "Is it like this everywhere?" That is all she could get out as the tears began to run down her cheeks swelled her throat shut to further words.

"I like to think that it isn't, but there are a few murders throughout the year where we live." Smitty's voice trailed off and he hoped she only heard the first part. "I'm driving back. You just rest. If they learn anything further, they will contact me."

"They did seem to know a few of the names. We can't prove it yet, but maybe they can find some evidence of a prior address." Aura spoke with a sad tone to her voice and wished they were already home. She was bored out of her mind. Not being a police officer, the men didn't let her see anything. "Why don't we drive around and maybe my dark angel will guide us to them." Suddenly inspired, Aura sat up and started watching around her and encouraged Smitty to make certain turns.

"If you make us too late, we will have to get a motel room." Smitty didn't like this idea because of the time, but it was an innovative idea. He hadn't been here in years and looked at the homes for where the older ones were.

"Once through and then home. It's worth a shot, huh." Aura said as she watched the homes they drove by.

Nearing the southern edge of the entire town, they drove by the town cemetery. As if she had predicted it, the mist rose up around Aura as a vision hit her harder than any had done so, ever before. A voice came out of it and Aura heard herself speak the words. "They are not here. Those you seek have gone to their deserved reward in the eternal fires that they caused in their lives."

Smitty wasn't expecting this and found himself swerving and fighting to regain control of the car as they screamed donuts but somehow did not destroy or hit anything surrounding them. He had just straightened out when he heard Aura speaking as if she never stopped.

"Return home and you will find them." A dark shadow swept through the car causing Smitty to brake hard to try and prevent further spinning but just managed to cause a worse disaster as they turned over and over down the street, landing on the wheels by some miraculous twist of fate. 'OMG' Smitty whispered just in case the shadow was an angel of God.

"What did you do?" Aura's own voice rang in his ears as she screamed to clear his head and her own.

"You wouldn't believe me if I told you. So, what did you learn?" Smitty felt his own heart pounding in his chest and thrumming in his ears. He took slow deep breaths as his vision began to close in and his head joined the throbbing of his ears by beginning to crush his brain.

"We need to go home. I think the angel was angry that we came here." Aura really didn't believe that angel's got angry but somehow this one did.

"You're kidding, right. I wanted to go home hours ago. Home, it is." Smitty was nearing a violent angry rage, but somehow, he managed to calm himself by the time they reached the highway again. He had a long drive ahead and no work results to show for today. His head was throbbing and so he kept silent. Aura had helped him and at least he had turned the list over to the locals. Tomorrow would take care of itself.

Chapter Twelve

Smitty was feeling good about the drive, they were nearing the last town before home when Aura sat up. "You, okay?" He asked but didn't get an answer. Knowing that she undoubtedly was having a vision, he became silent.

As they approached town, Aura pointed to the right and as he approached the first street off the road, she waved her hand frantically to the right. He turned, what choice did he have. He was having good result from her visions.

Smitty drove through town on a diagonal street that led him along the edge of town and eventually they were in the country. Aura was still sitting forward but hadn't moved a muscle other than to let her arm down to her right side.

Smitty wasn't surprised when Aura started whispering so low that the words could not be understood. She had done this before when the vision needed her to communicate. He just wished that she would speak up sooner and in a louder voice.

Aura for her part was in a fugue state. It is true that she whispered but it was the dark angel giving her guidance. She saw the road and knew it like the back of her hand, but she waited for a stop sign that was no longer there. As they turned to the right she screamed. "Stop!"

Smitty was disarmed by this scream as it deafened his hearing in his right ear, but he did not panic. Rather than dynamite his brakes, he slowed quickly. This police car could not handle another emergency stop. This still threw them forward, but their seatbelts saved them from serious harm. "What?"

Aura's left arm came up and pointed to the left. When she felt the car backing up, her arm swung forward but continued to point to the left.

Smitty was doubting his own sanity at this point and backed up the best he could with Aura's arm in front of his face. He stopped when he passed a turn off and put the car back into drive. He was beginning to shake at this point as his adrenaline level was already giving him palpitations and a migraine. He started driving forward at a slower rate in case they had to turn again.

Aura remained in her fugue state but had at least lowered her arm. A few hundred feet further, she loudly whispered, “Stop here at the cemetery. Dig in the back." With that, Aura leaned back against the seat and looked around. “Where are we?”

“An early cemetery from the looks of it. That’s my guess.” Smitty pulled up to the gate and stopped the car. “I want to hold your arm if we walk in there. You tend to faint without notice.” Smitty looked directly into Aura’s face and used his no nonsense voice to the best of his ability. He would have looked into her eyes, but she would not look at him.

“That would make me feel better, too.” Aura sighed and got out of the car. She walked around to the front of the car trying to find a way into the cemetery.

“Most people just walk through the hole next to the gate.” Smitty pointed and waited for Aura to go ahead of him because only one of them could go through this said hole at a time.

Aura didn’t want to be first, but she went into the house first and this was out in the open. She took small steps but walked through the hole expecting a specter to jump out of nowhere, none did.

"Watch out for blackberries, poison oak, poison ivy, devil's club and nettles." Smitty would be watching for them all, but he saw Aura turn around and start to leave. "It's all right. Mostly, it's just tall grass and a few burr weeds."

"Thanks, can we leave. Send your boys in to find graves without markers. Even then, those could be legitimate graves that had wooden markers, now long gone with the passage of time." Aura was angry now and walked into the cemetery on her own at this point. She was more worried about the real threats than the supernatural threats.

An hour later, the two returned to the car without any more information. "I think you are correct. We need to get the boys out here with their gear. You never saw a more beat up piece of machinery for the ground penetrating radar." Smitty closed his door and started the car.

"My helper didn't seem to want to help us tonight." Aura said it as a way of apology. She didn't feel responsible but was beginning to think like the spirit.

The drive home was silent and emotionally cold. Neither of the car's occupants was feeling chatty. Smitty parked in front of Aura's house, and she let herself out. The only sound was the door opening and closing. Even her steps were silent as she walked away due to her new soft soled shoes.

Smitty drove away wondering if there was another way to catch their villains without digging up the bodies first. He was nearly home when it occurred to him that a stakeout of the cemetery might be in order. He shivered as he realized how many days the stakeout might take to fulfill his need. In the morning, he would talk it over with his captain.

Chapter Thirteen

Morning found Detective Smitty waiting for his Captain to appear. He was unable to sleep for more than two hours and made himself a pot of strong coffee. He brought a thermos in as well as his to go mug. He drank three mugs before his captain appeared and he was feeling incredibly positive about his potential pitch to his captain. He decided a stakeout might actually work.

"Captain?" Smitty started but his captain had obviously seen this coming and interrupted him.

"Whatever it is, no. We don't have the budget for it." With that the Captain shut his door blocking Smitty from entering.

Smitty sullenly walked over to his own desk. He kept a box under it at all times, just in case. It only took a couple of minutes, and he was ready to leave. As he walked away, his weapon and shield lay silently on his desk. He felt as if they were drilling a hole in his back and calling him to change his mind. He would not be doing that. He had enough time in to retire and this kind of stakeout would take more hours than he could do in his off time. He was committed to finding the people who thought they got away with mass murder and kidnapping. They were ghosts and he was a ghost hunter.

A month later, Smitty was laying in his camo-sleep area eating an egg salad sandwich brought to him a week ago by Aura. She thought he was 'nuts' but joined him occasionally. There had been no sign of anyone and eventually, Aura stopped coming except to bring him a new cooler of food.

Smitty had decided this would be his last night. In the morning he would call and bring in ground searchers. It wouldn't help but at least he could bring closure to the illegally buried.

His last bite consumed; he swallowed it dry. The last of his coffee was long gone. This would be a long night of trying to stay awake. He looked around as far as he could see in the near pitch dark constantly moving his eyes. He had never seen any movement but there were sounds of animals passing that he safely ignored.

Smitty had definitely become bored, and he was very tired. Eventually, he slept lighter than usual. In the middle of a wild dream of sorts, he snapped awake. He had heard something. He somehow managed to remain quiet and lay down as he surveyed the open area in front of him. Why couldn't there be a moon of any size? He was on his second sweep of his field of vision when he saw the people. Men probably. They were carrying black plastic items, wrapped in plastic, and bound with cord or rope. They were on the far side of the cemetery as he mentally had predicted.

Smitty started crawling around on the very edge of the cemetery where he had been for the last month. He double clicked his walkie and hoped someone was awake. His walkie was turned off, but the buttons would still activate anyone else's walkie. He hoped they were awake and, on the way, to offer assistance.

Without waiting for help, Smitty continued his approach heading for the people he observed and tried to listen for any conversation. When he was within one hundred feet, he began to hear occasional talking. He guessed they didn't talk when they dug because he could clearly see the two people digging and throwing dirt his way.

Cursing nonverbally, Smitty began crawling further into the cemetery because no one could get into the dense bushes. When he was past the flying dirt, Smitty again started to crawl toward the men. He only had about fifty feet left to go when he heard sirens coming, finally.

The people turned toward the sirens and their faces were revealed to Smitty who was now hiding behind the last upright headstone before the end of the known cemetery. Smitty now knew they were men and in fact recognized one of them. He was a small-time thief and bag man from town. The other one was a mystery and nearly three times as old as the boy that Smitty recognized.

The two men resumed digging at a faster rate and Smitty remained behind the tombstone until the sirens brought help a lot closer. When he heard gravel flying and hitting the metal of the cruiser's undercarriage, Smitty stood up and yelled, "You are both under arrest. Stand where you are with your hands behind your heads." He could hear officer's behind him saying much the same thing.

The two men looked around as if about to flee, but there were officers coming up behind them. In minutes, they were cuffed and led off to a cruiser.

'Now to get them to confess.' Smitty thought to himself as he walked over to where the items to be buried lay. "Find anything incriminating?"

"Not unless you think that a dead dog is a reason." The officer with gloves on was inspecting the contents of the bags. "Oh, and here's a bag of assorted dead animals. Up and coming serial killer, I'd say." He stood up as he said this and looking into Smitty's eyes, fighting to keep the smile off of his face.

"To true, but I suppose I should ask after their parents and grandparents." Smitty snapped back and turned to walk to his car. He would need to get over to the local station and listen in on the interrogation.

Smitty walked into the station intending to ask permission to listen in. What he met was the Captain walking away from a closed interrogation room door. "Done already?"

"You could say that. He asked for a lawyer. Knappe is in court and won't be here for an hour or so. Would you like some coffee?" The Captain pointed to the half full coffee pot and walked into his office, meaning, help yourself.

Chapter Fourteen

Morning found Smitty waking up to find that it was now afternoon. He got up muttering under his breath about the time and his tardiness. He nearly skipped a shower but caught a whiff of himself and took a quick one while waiting for the coffee to brew.

His clothes went on with difficulty because he wasn't completely dry. He walked past the coffee on his way out and snagged his to go cup, already filled because he only made a small amount today. Sipping on his coffee he walked out to his car for a short drive to his office. He had days of paperwork to do but mostly he wanted to talk to the two men from yesterday.

He was glad that his Captain never put through his termination papers. He still had a job, and his captain even paid him for eighty hours of stake-out.

Smitty was only two feet into the building when he saw his Captain looking grim and waving to him. 'This isn't good.' Smitty thought to himself. Walking over to where his Captain stood waiting for him, he spoke before he reached him. "What happened?"

"We had to release them because someone paid the fine for attempting to dispose of animal remains in an illegal fashion." The Captain's voice carried enough anger undertone to light a fire in the rain as he spoke his answer and then left.

Smitty cursed to himself and went to find the names and addresses of the people arrested and those who paid the bail. This was all he had, and he wasn't going to lose this, too.

A week later, Smitty went to his Captain with the current information he had found. His Captain didn't like information on a daily blow by blow fashion, unless it had a huge impact. He wasn't in, but Smitty knew what needed to be done and left a note for his Captain with a copy of the information.

'I've started a stake out of these addresses. We need to find out if they have more women captive and where they are being kept.'

As he walked out of the office, Smitty shuttered as the feeling of being on the carpet again settled over him. He might not get paid for this, but he had rented an apartment that overlooked two of the addresses. He was on his way to pick up cameras and other surveillance equipment. It would take time, but he was determined.

It took a few days and pulling in a lot of markers from past favors for Smitty to get more officers to assist with the surveillance. He asked for and was given the night shift. As he sat in the apartment watching those who came and went, he wondered what they were up to and why. How could they feel right about what they were doing? The only answer he ever came up with is they no longer felt anything. Greed had clouded their eyes to the reality of what they were doing to the human beings in front of them. After a while, he stopped thinking about it and just focused on finding a way to end this as fast as he could.

The first month went by and only the two men came and went. Smitty was beginning to think they needed to move on. He spent his copious time making possible lists of places they could be keeping the women and other hostages.

Stopping what he was doing, Smitty looked up and grabbed his binoculars. A large moving van just pulled up in front of their hide out. Across the street from Smitty. It blocked his line of sight to the front door, and this was not acceptable.

Grabbing his walkie and the binoculars, Smitty left the stake-out site with everyone else on his heels. As he ran down along the corridors, he attempted to raise help on the walkie. Stopping at the top of the stairs, he clicked on his walkie. "This is Alpha to Omega. Everyone to the Alpha site, now." With that, he pocketed the walkie and headed down the stairs. He patted himself down to verify that he had his chosen weapons, and he did. With two extra clips in each pocket, and his vest under his shirt, Smitty was as ready as he could be.

Chapter Fifteen

Minutes later, Smitty stood hidden in a bush up close to the front door. He was waiting for a mic click for each group of volunteer officers who were here to rescue and arrest as the case may be. Time slowed and Smitty's breathing seemed non-existent. He needed to breathe, his vision was going, and he needed to breathe.

Finally, a click and then more. When all the groups clicked in, Smitty waved them forward and gave a final double click to the mic as he began moving forward.

Smitty was the second one in and they yelled, "Police." As they walked through the house with their guns pointed straight ahead, Smitty worried about accidentally shooting the man in front of him.

There was no sound in the house, but the van was outside, still, and there were occupants, and everyone knew that. They had all seen them come inside through the very door that they came in. Slowly, they progressed through the home but found no one home.

Two officers progressed upstairs but returned to the main floor having found no one home. A cursory search of the main floor did not show any access to a basement, but they went around again. This time they looked under every rug and behind every bookcase and into the closets looking for doors in the walls and ceilings and floors.

"Found it!" came a call from one of the closets. Everyone followed the sound and there in the back of this closet was another room and a set of stairs.

"Right. Single file and keep your eyes open." Smitty took the lead this time because he was the most experienced and knew how to keep a sharp eye out. He hoped they were bad shots, and he could duck back if the shooting did begin.

At the bottom of the stairs, they could visually see the room around them was also empty of people. There was garbage and empty furniture and dressers with no drawers because the drawers were spread around the room. "Someone packed in a hurry." Smitty said and motioned for them to split up and search the hallways.

As they split off, Smitty took the left of three access hallways, and he could hear the others beginning to search their chosen corridors. Smitty was beginning to worry that somehow, they had escaped.

An hour later found the group retreating from the building. Smitty continued on out the back tunnel and eventually found himself in the basement of another building. He silently used several expletives; he knew he had lost them. It took another fifteen minutes for him to find an exit on the main floor that wasn't locked from the inside.

As Smitty emerged from the building, he could see his own car and headed in that direction. Just then, the van began moving and he ran for his car and put the walkie to his mouth. "They are in the van and it's leaving!"

As much as Smitty tried to run faster, the van was out of sight by the time his car started and moving. He drove down the way he last saw the van and zig-zagged through the streets. He saw other officer's doing the same but expected they had lost their chance.

After about a half an hour without a sighting, Smitty headed back to the office just as the walkie clicked on. "Van sighted at the last corner leaving town on the north side. Out."

"Lucky." Smitty smiled and turned around to find the last known location. There were many ways out of town, but only a couple of them could be reached from this location.

Smitty drove out of town but could not see a van or a police undercover vehicle. He began picking up speed slightly and Smitty continued on out of his jurisdiction and into hot water if someone pulled him over for speeding. Up ahead he could see something was stopping and backing up traffic. Turning on his lights and siren, Smitty slowed to allow people to pull aside.

Slowly, Smitty drove through the traffic hoping this was a blockage created to stop the van. It was not, but it worked just the same. Up ahead of him, he could now see the van and radioed in for help. He began improvising a plan in his head as he drove up behind the van.

Clearly, the van was as stuck as everyone else and could not yield the right of way to a police car or anyone else. Smitty finally was forced to stop. He got out and began walking forward. As he did so, he pulled his weapon and tried to move into the blind spot behind every large van or big rig. He was on his own and he knew it.

He could hear people calling to him and he motioned them to get down, but otherwise ignored them for everyone's safety.

Half a mile ahead, a quarter mile from the scene of the accident, another officer worked his way from car to car checking on the occupants and sending for assistance where needed. He heard the siren and vaguely saw the light because it wasn't dark enough to be certain. He thought it was assistance arriving and wondered why they were coming through the snarled mess of traffic.

When the siren went silent, he looked up to see why. This is when his instincts clicked in. He forgot about the accident, worried more about a possible shooting. Pulling his weapon, but holding it behind his back, the officer began to walk through the crumpled mess of cars and crying victims.

It was in this way the the two officers began to converge on the van that now lay between them. The officers only got about a car length closer before they saw movement inside of the cab. The men were armed and getting out.

Just as they saw this and ducked behind the closest vehicle with the car's occupants, a sudden wind blew in out of nowhere. All of the road debris followed the vortex as it viciously aimed itself only at the cab of the van. The men struggled to get out, but the doors were repeatedly slammed shut after even the smallest attempt at opening the doors.

The van occupants were so focused on getting out that they failed to remember their guns. Before anyone knew it, the two officers pulled open the doors and arrested the occupants.

As they were doing the arresting, the back door flew open allowing the women inside to get a breath of fresh air without debris now that the vortex suddenly disappeared. Somewhere along the way, Smitty's reinforcements showed up and began removing the women and girls from the back.

The tow trucks arrived and began clearing the multi car wreck from in front of the van. Smitty helped to put his arrestee into the back of the other officer's cruiser and the officer put his arrestee into the back of a fellow officer's cruiser where they left them to sweat out their stories.

The sky was clear today and now that the sun was up, the officers would have to leave soon with the arrested men. The inside of the cruisers would be heating up.

Smitty walked around overseeing the release of the women and awaiting an oversized tow truck with a crane specially designed to remove this van from the freeway. Eventually, the inner lane was cleared to allow the backed-up traffic to begin dissipating. A couple of officers handled the traffic as they encouraged the three lanes to merge in a more or less organized disorganization that would allow everyone to move away from the van and looky-loo vantage.

Smitty realized then that his car was in the middle of the melee and moved toward it trying to stay alive. As he got inside and shut his door for the first time in a very long time, a gust of wind moved past him and he clearly heard words coming with the air. 'Thank-you and say good-bye to Aura.'

Smiling, Smitty started his car and waiting his turn to move over to the inside lane. These officer's had the situation under control, and he had a lot of paperwork to do. Maybe he would retire and leave this to the younger generation.

Aura

Made in the USA
Columbia, SC
28 July 2023